MW00976949

Walk the Plank, Plankton

Barnacle Barb & Her Pirate Crew

Written by Nadia Higgins
Illustrated by Jimmy Holder

magic Wagon

For my mother, my most careful reader

visit us at www.abdopublishing.com

Published by Magic Wagon, a division of the ABDO Publishing Group, 8000 West 78th Street, Edina, Minnesota 55439.
Copyright © 2008 by Abdo Consulting Group, Inc. International copyrights reserved in all countries. All rights reserved.
No part of this book may be reproduced in any form without written permission from the publisher.
Looking Glass Library™ is a trademark and logo of Magic Wagon.

Printed in the United States.

Text by Nadia Higgins
Illustrations by Jimmy Holder
Edited by Bob Temple
Interior layout and design by Emily Love
Cover design by Emily Love

Library of Congress Cataloging-in-Publication Data
Higgins, Nadia.
  Walk the plank, Plankton / Nadia Higgins ; illustrated by Jimmy Holder.
    p. cm. — (Barnacle Barb & her pirate crew)
  ISBN 978-1-60270-094-9
  [1. Pirates—Fiction. 2. Dinosaurs—Fiction.] I. Holder, Jimmy, ill. II. Title.
PZ7.H5349558Wal 2008
[E]—dc22
                              2007036975

It was a sunny Saturday morning aboard the pirate ship. The decks were filled with whistling, clinking, scraping, and other happy pirate noises.

Armpit Arnie was beating Slimebeard at a game of "Go Shark," while Stinkin' Jim picked fleas off Billy the parrot. In the kitchen, Shrimp-Breath Sherman stirred a pot of cocktail sauce.

Barnacle Barb and Pegleg Pedro stretched out on their lounge chairs.

"Saturday," Pegleg sighed, "as lovely as a rainbow trout."

"Here! Here!" Barb joined in. "The best day of the—"

Faster than she could say "week," a band of enemy pirates stormed the ship.

"Attack! Attack!" Pegleg Pedro cried. The crew rushed forward. "Load the cannons! Swashbuckle ye swords!" Barnacle Barb barked.

"Don't bother!" a growly voice called out through the cannon smoke.

"Uggghhh," the pirates groaned at the sound of the familiar voice.

"'Tis Plankton Petunia and her band of bumbling buccaneers," Barb sighed.

"Aye, 'tis I," Plankton snarled. "And we've got you now! Fetch the treasure," she ordered one of her buccaneers.

Barnacle Barb winked at Pegleg Pedro. "I'll keep her distracted," she whispered.

"Yoo-hoo, Plankton!" Barb called.

"What now?" Plankton Petunia snapped.

"Oh, me hearty, have you heard the latest joke about Tri-scare-atops?" Barb asked.

"No!" In spite of herself, Plankton giggled in anticipation. "Tell, tell, tell!" she squealed.

Everyone the high seas over knew that Plankton Petunia was crazy about dinosaurs. Instead of the usual skull and crossbones, her ship's flag showed dinosaur fossils. She always had all the dinosaur books checked out of the library. And for Pirate Fair one year, she'd won a blue ribbon for her report on giant ferns.

"Well, a Tri-scare-atops and a pirate walk into gym class . . . ," Barb began.

As Barnacle Barb kept Plankton Petunia's attention, Pegleg Pedro caught up with the bumbling buccaneer sent after the treasure.

Down in the hold, Pegleg tapped the buccaneer on the shoulder. "Please, allow me," he said, pointing to the treasure.

"Arrrgh, thank goodness," the buccaneer said, stretching out on an old sandbag. Pegleg pretended to scoop up the treasure, and soon the buccaneer was fast asleep. Pegleg gently lifted his snoring enemy into a rowboat and pushed him out to sea.

"Now, for the secret weapon," Pegleg said.

When Pegleg Pedro poked his head up on deck, Plankton Petunia was howling with laughter. The coast was clear, so he hoisted up a giant picture.

"Pssssst," he called to Armpit Arnie. "Help me hold this up." The two pirates held the picture out over the ship's rails. Then, they waited for the buccaneers to notice it.

Sure enough, the enemy pirates started racing toward the sign. And as they raced, they started fighting. Soon, they were throwing each other overboard.

"What do you call a dinosaur stuck in a glacier?" Barnacle Barb continued. "A fossicle!"

Plankton Petunia's whole crew was gone, and she was rolling on the floor with laughter. As quietly as an ocean tide, Barb crouched down and tied Plankton's shoelaces together.

"Another one! Another one!" Plankton said, gasping for air.

"What did Barnacle Barrrb say to Plankton Petunia?" Barb asked.

Plankton looked up. "What?"

"Walk the plank, Plankton!" Barb hooted.

Plankton sat up. She looked around. "Curses!" she hollered. "That bumbling bunch of bubbleheads!"

Pegleg Pedro sneered. Slimebeard snarled. Armpit Arnie scoffed, and Shrimp-Breath Sherman growled.

But Stinkin' Jim looked down. He made a circle in the dust with his toe. *"Don't notice me. Don't notice me,"* he chanted in his head.

Though not many people knew it, Stinkin' was almost as crazy about dinosaurs as Plankton Petunia. Like her, he had his own collection of dinosaur things. It included a Velociraptor feather pen, a Stegosaurus snow globe, and glow-in-the-dark stickers of Pterodactyl, Apatosaurus, and Protoceratops, just to name a few.

In fact, Stinkin' and Plankton were pen pals. They had written many times about their dinosaur collections. Of course, Stinkin' never signed his real name. His mates aboard ship would be shocked to know that he was known to Plankton Petunia—their greatest enemy—as "Dinosaur Fan Number Two."

"Think. Think," Stinkin' Jim muttered while the others lowered the plank. "That's it!" he hissed.

"My, my, my," Stinkin' said loudly. He strutted over to the group. "Look at the time." He pointed at the sundial. "Only 20 minutes until the new Starfish Wars movie starts."

The pirates gasped. Barnacle Barb smacked her forehead. "It completely slipped me mind!" she said. "What with the enemy attack and all."

"We'll be missing the previews if we don't go RIGHT THIS SECOND!" Slimebeard cried.

The pirates didn't know what to do. They looked at Plankton Petunia.

"Uh … um … arrrgh," Stinkin' Jim said, trying to find his meanest pirate voice. "I'll guard the prisoner while yer gone."

"Three cheers for Stinkin'!" the other pirates cried. Then they gathered up their coins, eye patches, and warm sweaters and headed for the movies.

Stinkin' explained everything to Plankton Petunia as he untied her shoelaces.

"Dinosaur Fan Number Two?!" Plankton could hardly believe it. "Show me yer Velociraptor feather pen! Show me yer Stegosaurus snow globe!" Her feet now free, she danced a little jig.

Stinkin' Jim led Plankton Petunia to his secret collection under his hammock. Plankton gently picked up and examined each item.

"A real Allosaurus tooth?" she exclaimed.

"Nah, 'tis just a copy," Stinkin' replied.

"Still, 'tis cool," Plankton said, reaching for Stinkin's copy of *The Encyclopedia of Prehistoric Parrots*.

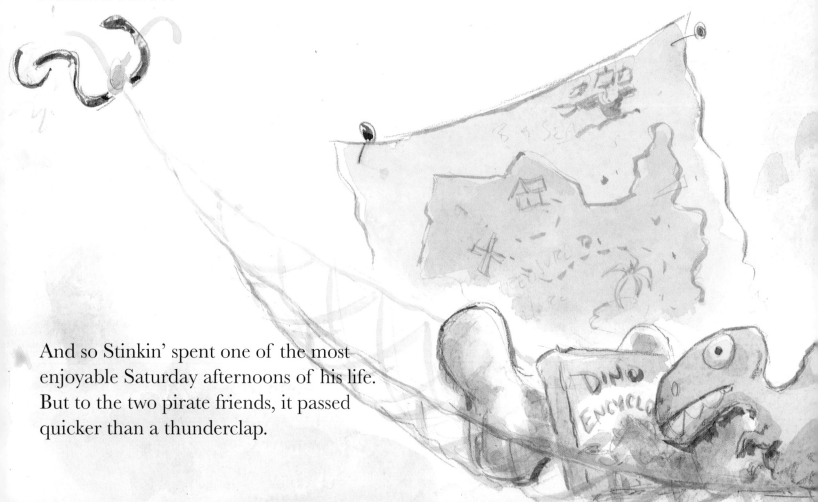

And so Stinkin' spent one of the most enjoyable Saturday afternoons of his life. But to the two pirate friends, it passed quicker than a thunderclap.

"Arrrgh," Stinkin' Jim said, pointing to the sun dipping in the sky. "I suppose the mates will be coming back now."

"We should be gettin' back to the plank," Plankton Petunia suggested. She understood that, as a pirate, her new friend could never, ever let her go.

"Here," she said, once they were on deck, "let me do that." And so Plankton Petunia tied her shoelaces back together just as the crew returned.

What happened next was like a dream to Stinkin' Jim. He watched as if in a trance as the crew got Plankton Petunia all tied up for her plank walk.

"Do something! Do something! Do something!" he shouted to himself in his head. *"Do sommmmmme-thiiiiiing!!!!"*

"Aha!" Stinkin' snapped out his trance.

"I'll be right back!" he shouted. "I'm uh . . . I'll be back with more rope!" he lied. But his mates were too excited about the plank walk to even notice he was gone.

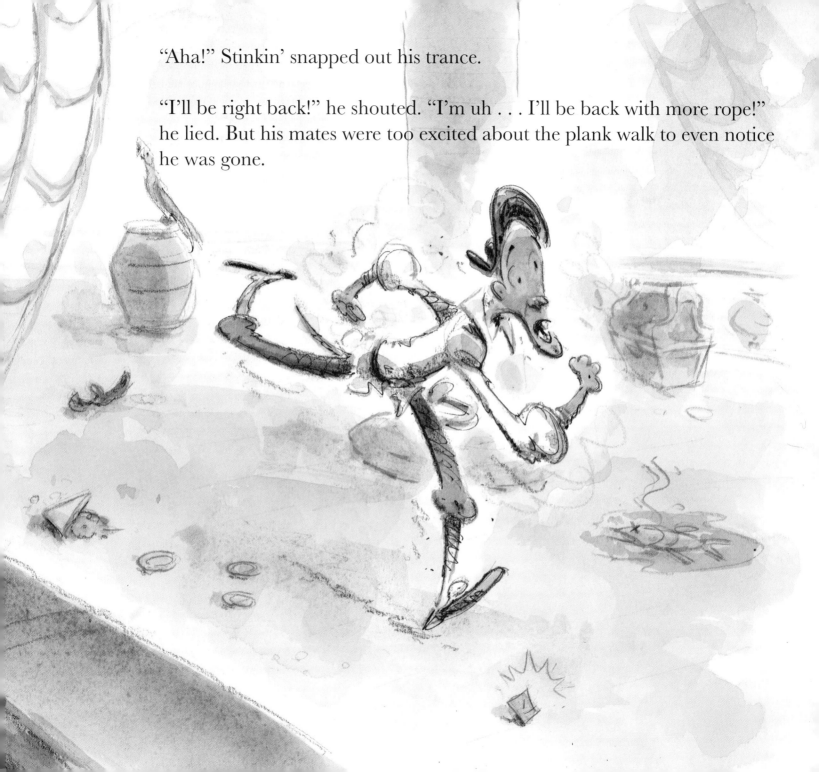

Crouching under his hammock, Stinkin' Jim sifted through his dinosaur collection. "Where is it? Where is it?" he muttered, scattering fossils and eggshells and plastic dinosaur parts all over the place.

At last he found it—his T. Rex Floatie still in its original box.

Stinkin' ran to the peephole. He looked up. There was the plank right above him.

Stinkin' pulled out the floppy, rubber tube and crammed it through the peephole. Then, the pirate blew and blew as hard as a puffer fish.

Creak. Creak. Creak.

Above, Plankton Petunia was stepping down the plank.

Stinkin' Jim knew he was out of time. He stopped blowing. He plugged the tube. He held out his dinosaur floatie with both hands, and he closed his eyes.

Swoosh.

All of a sudden, the inner tube felt heavy. Stinkin' let go. After a long time, he opened his eyes.

There was his inner tube. And there was Plankton Petunia floating away inside it. His plan had worked!

"Ahoy!" Stinkin' waved to Plankton. She smiled back. Then, Stinkin' sat down to write Plankton a message in a bottle.

"*Dear Plankton,*" he wrote. "*I'm glad ye didn't drown. Would ye like to go to the new Jurassic Shark movie with me?*"

Stinkin' Jim looked out his window. Plankton Petunia was just a speck at sea.

He continued, "*Sincerely yours, Dinosaur Fan . . .*"

"No, no, no," he muttered. He crossed out the last line.

Stinkin' picked up his Velociraptor feather pen. Then, for the first time ever, he finished a letter to Plankton Petunia with, "*Your friend, Stinkin' Jim.*"

Pirate Booty

- In the age of pirates, all ships flew flags. Naval ships and trading vessels had flags showing which country they belonged to. Pirates also designed flags, or Jolly Rogers, that let their enemies know exactly who was approaching.

- Pirates rarely fired cannons to attack their enemies. Instead, they quickly boarded a ship, took the booty on board, and retreated.

- *Pirate* is only one word for these rough sea robbers. *Buccaneers* is another word for pirates. So are *freebooters*, *picaroons*, and *sea rovers*.

Pirate Translations

ahoy — hello
aye — ouch, or yes
jig — dance
mate — friend
swashbuckle — wave one's sword about while looking fierce
walk the plank — die